I thought I saw a

by Dugald Steer Illustrated by Lucy Maddison

mustard

I'm going on a ghost hunt.
I'm off to spot a spook.

They say that ghosts are scary,
I say GOBBLEDEGOOK!

I'm setting off at midnight,
I'll climb the dark hillside.

I know a creepy castle,
I wonder who's inside?

I know a scary station,
With a track they'll never mend.

If you see the train that stops there,
Your hair will stand on end.

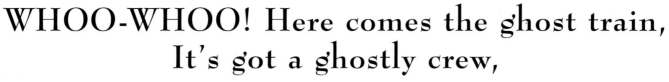

WHOO-WHOO! Here comes the ghost train,
It's got a ghostly crew,

It's full of phantom passengers –
Do ghosts like these scare you?

I know an eerie mansion,
It's dark and damp and cold.

A ghostly family live inside
They're very, VERY old!

There's Mr. Fright the father,
And nasty Mrs. Fear,

And Nick and Beth, the ghastly twins.
You'd shake if they came near.

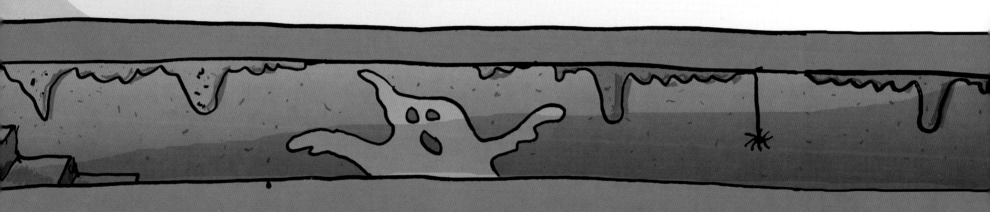

And down deep in the cellar,
Ghostly children like to play.

They'll pull all sorts of faces,
To frighten you away.

...AND SCARE THE PHANTOMS BACK!